I0452523

NUMBER 13

-FANTASY AND HORROR CLASSICS-

BY

M. R. JAMES

Copyright © 2013 Read Books Ltd.
This book is copyright and may not be
reproduced or copied in any way without
the express permission of the publisher in writing

British Library Cataloguing-in-Publication Data
A catalogue record for this book is available from the
British Library

M. R. James

Montague Rhodes James was born in Kent, England in 1862. An intellectually gifted child, he excelled academically at both Temple Grove School and Eton College before enrolling at King's College, Cambridge. A highly respected scholar to this day, James' areas of research interest were apocryphal Biblical literature and mediaeval illuminated manuscripts. He was, by turns, Fellow, Dean, and Tutor at King's College, and in 1905 was installed as Provost. James was a highly sociable man, and he travelled widely throughout Europe.

James came to writing fiction relatively late, not publishing his first collection of short stories – Ghost Stories of an Antiquary (1904) – until the age of 42. Many of his tales were written as Christmas Eve entertainments and read aloud to friends. James described his introduction to ghosts in 1931: "In my childhood I chanced to see a toy Punch and Judy set, with figures cut out in cardboard. One of these was The Ghost. It was a tall figure habited in white with an unnaturally long and narrow head, also surrounded with white, and a dismal visage. Upon this my conceptions of a ghost were based, and for years it permeated my dreams." James believed that must a good story must "put the reader into the position of saying to himself: 'If I'm not careful, something of this kind may happen to me!'" He eventually published five collections of his ghost stories, all of which were reprinted and adapted numerous times.

Modern scholars now see James as having redefined the ghost story for the 20th century by abandoning many of the formal Gothic clichés of his predecessors and using more realistic contemporary settings. However, James's tales tend to reflect his own antiquarian interests, and he is seen as the founder of the 'antiquarian ghost story'. His first two collections – Ghost Stories of an Antiquary (1904) and More Ghost Stories (1911) – are generally regarded as his most important, containing as they do the well-known stories 'Number 13', 'Count Magnus', 'Oh, Whistle and I'll Come to You, My Lad' and 'Casting the Runes'.

The onset of World War One marked the beginning of the end of James' golden years in Cambridge. In 1918, he accepted the post of Provost of Eton College. He was awarded the Order of Merit in 1930, and died in 1936, aged 73.

NUMBER 13

Among the towns of Jutland, Viborg justly holds a high place. It is the seat of a bishopric; it has a handsome but almost entirely new cathedral, a charming garden, a lake of great beauty, and many storks. Near it is Hald, accounted one of the prettiest things in Denmark; and hard by is Finderup, where Marsk Stig murdered King Erik Glipping on St Cecilia's Day, in the year 1286. Fifty-six blows of square-headed iron maces were traced on Erik's skull when his tomb was opened in the seventeenth century. But I am not writing a guide-book.

There are good hotels in Viborg—Preisler's and the Phoenix are all that can be desired. But my cousin, whose experiences I have to tell you now, went to the Golden Lion the first time that he visited Viborg. He has not been there since, and the following pages will, perhaps, explain the reason of his abstention.

The Golden Lion is one of the very few houses in the town that were not destroyed in the great fire of 1726, which practically demolished the cathedral, the Sognekirke, the Raadhuus, and so much else that was old and interesting. It is a great red-brick house—that is, the front is of brick, with corbie steps on the gables and a text over the door; but the courtyard into which the omnibus drives is of black and white wood and plaster.

The sun was declining in the heavens when my cousin walked up to the door, and the light smote full upon the imposing façade of the house. He was delighted with the old-fashioned aspect of the place, and promised himself a thoroughly satisfactory and amusing stay in an inn so typical of old Jutland.

It was not business in the ordinary sense of the word that had brought Mr Anderson to Viborg. He was engaged upon some researches into the Church history of Denmark, and it had come to his knowledge that in the Rigsarkiv of Viborg there were papers, saved from the fire, relating to the last days of Roman Catholicism in the country. He proposed, therefore, to spend a considerable time—perhaps as much as a fortnight or three weeks—in examining and copying these, and he hoped that the Golden Lion would be able to give him a room of sufficient size to serve alike as a bedroom and a study. His wishes were explained to the landlord, and, after a certain amount of thought, the latter suggested that perhaps it might be the best way for the gentleman to look at one or two of the larger rooms and pick one for himself. It seemed a good idea.

The top floor was soon rejected as entailing too much getting upstairs after the day's work; the second floor contained no room of exactly the dimensions required; but on the first floor there was a choice of two or three rooms which would, so far as size went, suit admirably.

The landlord was strongly in favour of Number 17, but Mr Anderson pointed out that its windows commanded only the blank wall of the next house, and that it would be very dark in the afternoon. Either Number 12 or Number 14 would be better, for both of them looked on the street, and the bright evening light and the pretty view would more than compensate him for the additional amount of noise.

Eventually Number 12 was selected. Like its neighbours, it had three windows, all on one side of the room; it was fairly high and unusually long. There was, of course, no fireplace, but the stove was handsome and rather old—a cast-iron erection, on the side of which was a representation of Abraham sacrificing Isaac, and the inscription, 'I Bog Mose, Cap. 22,' above. Nothing else in the room was remarkable; the only interesting picture was an old coloured print of the town, date about 1820.

Supper-time was approaching, but when Anderson, refreshed by the ordinary ablutions, descended the staircase, there were still a few minutes before the bell rang. He devoted them to examining the list of his fellow-lodgers. As is usual in Denmark, their names were displayed on a large blackboard, divided into columns and lines, the numbers of the rooms being painted in at the beginning of each line. The list was not exciting. There was an advocate, or Sagförer, a German, and some bagmen from Copenhagen. The one and only point which suggested any food for thought was the absence of any Number 13 from the tale of the rooms, and even this was a thing which Anderson had already noticed half a dozen times in his experience of Danish hotels. He could not help wondering whether the objection to that particular number, common as it is, was so widespread and so strong as to make it difficult to let a room so ticketed, and he resolved to ask the landlord if he and his colleagues in the profession had actually met with many clients who refused to be accommodated in the thirteenth room.

He had nothing to tell me (I am giving the story as I heard it from him) about what passed at supper, and the evening, which was spent in unpacking and arranging his clothes, books, and papers, was not more eventful. Towards eleven o'clock he resolved to go to bed, but with him, as with a good many other people nowadays, an almost necessary preliminary to bed, if he meant to sleep, was the reading of a few pages of print, and he now remembered that the particular book which he had been reading in the train, and which alone would satisfy him at that present moment, was in the pocket of his great-coat, then hanging on a peg outside the dining-room.

To run down and secure it was the work of a moment, and, as the passages were by no means dark, it was not difficult for him to find his way back to his own door. So, at least, he thought; but when he arrived there, and turned the handle, the door entirely refused to open, and he caught the sound of a hasty movement towards it from within. He had tried the wrong door, of course. Was his own room to the right or to the left? He glanced at the number: it was 13. His room would be on the left; and so it was. And not before he had been in bed for some minutes, had read his wonted three or four pages of his book, blown out his light, and turned over to go to sleep, did it occur to him that, whereas on the blackboard of the hotel there had been no Number 13, there was undoubtedly a room numbered 13 in the hotel. He felt rather sorry he had not chosen it for his own. Perhaps he might have done the landlord a little service by occupying it, and given him the chance of saying that a well-born English gentleman had lived in it for three weeks and liked it very much. But probably it was used as a servant's room or something of the kind. After all, it was most likely not so large or good a room as his own. And he looked drowsily about the room, which was fairly perceptible in the half-light from the street-lamp. It was a curious effect, he thought. Rooms usually look larger in a dim light than a full one, but this seemed to have contracted in length and grown proportionately higher. Well, well! sleep was more important than these vague ruminations—and to sleep he went.

On the day after his arrival Anderson attacked the Rigsarkiv of Viborg. He was, as one might expect in Denmark, kindly received, and access to all that he wished to see was made as easy for him as possible. The documents laid before him were far more numerous and interesting than he had at all anticipated. Besides official papers, there was a large bundle of correspondence relating to Bishop Jörgen Friis, the last Roman Catholic who held the see, and in these there cropped up many amusing and what are called 'intimate' details of private life and individual character. There was much talk of a house owned by the Bishop, but not inhabited by him, in the town. Its tenant was apparently somewhat of a scandal and a stumbling-block to the reforming party. He was a disgrace, they wrote, to the city; he practised secret and wicked arts, and had sold his soul to the enemy. It was of a piece with the gross corruption and superstition of the Babylonish Church that such a viper and blood-sucking Troldmand should be patronized and harboured by the Bishop. The Bishop met these reproaches boldly; he protested his own abhorrence of all such things as secret arts, and required his antagonists to bring the matter before the proper court—of course, the spiritual court—and sift it to the bottom. No one could be more ready and willing than himself to condemn Mag Nicolas Francken if the evidence showed him to have been guilty of any of the crimes informally alleged against him.

Anderson had not time to do more than glance at the next letter of the Protestant leader, Rasmus Nielsen, before the record office was closed for the day, but he gathered its general tenor, which was to the effect that Christian men were now no longer bound by the decisions of Bishops of Rome, and that the Bishop's Court was not, and could not be, a fit or competent tribunal to judge so grave and weighty a cause.

On leaving the office, Mr Anderson was accompanied by the old gentleman who presided over it, and, as they walked, the conversation very naturally turned to the papers of which I have just been speaking.

Herr Scavenius, the Archivist of Viborg, though very well informed as to the general run of the documents under his charge, was not a specialist in those of the Reformation period. He was much interested in what Anderson had to tell him about them. He looked forward with great pleasure, he said, to seeing the publication in which Mr Anderson spoke of embodying their contents. 'This house of the Bishop Friis,' he added, 'it is a great puzzle to me where it can have stood. I have studied carefully the topography of old Viborg, but it is most unlucky—of the old terrier of the Bishop's property which was made in 1560, and of which we have the greater part in the Arkiv—just the piece which had the list of the town property is missing. Never mind. Perhaps I shall some day succeed to find him.'

After taking some exercise—I forget exactly how or where—Anderson went back to the Golden Lion, his supper, his game of patience, and his bed. On the way to his room it occurred to him that he had forgotten to talk to the landlord about the omission of Number 13 from the hotel board, and also that he might as well make sure that Number 13 did actually exist before he made any reference to the matter.

The decision was not difficult to arrive at. There was the door with its number as plain as could be, and work of some kind was evidently going on inside it, for as he neared the door he could hear footsteps and voices, or a voice, within. During the few seconds in which he halted to make sure of the number, the footsteps ceased, seemingly very near the door, and he was a little startled at hearing a quick hissing breathing as of a person in strong excitement. He went on to his own room, and again he was surprised to find how much smaller it seemed now than it had when he selected it. It was a slight disappointment, but only slight. If he found it really not large enough, he could very easily shift to another. In the meantime he wanted something—as far as I remember it was a pocket-handkerchief—out of his portmanteau, which had been placed by the porter on a very inadequate trestle or stool against the wall at the farthest end of the room from his bed. Here was a very curious thing: the portmanteau was not to be seen. It had been moved by officious servants; doubtless the contents had been put in the wardrobe. No, none of them were there. This was vexatious. The idea of a theft he dismissed at once. Such things rarely happen in Denmark, but some piece of stupidity had certainly been performed (which is not so uncommon), and the stuepige must be severely spoken to. Whatever it was that he wanted, it was not so necessary to his comfort that he could not wait till the morning for it, and he therefore settled not to ring the bell and disturb the servants. He went to the window— the right-hand window it was—and looked out on the quiet street. There was a tall building opposite, with large spaces of dead wall; no passers-by; a dark night; and very little to be seen of any kind.

The light was behind him, and he could see his own shadow clearly cast on the wall opposite. Also the shadow of the bearded man in Number 11 on the left, who passed to and fro in shirtsleeves once or twice, and was seen first brushing his hair, and later on in a nightgown. Also the shadow of the occupant of Number 13 on the right. This might be more interesting. Number 13 was, like himself, leaning on his elbows on the window-sill looking out into the street. He seemed to be a tall thin man—or was it by any chance a woman?—at least, it was someone who covered his or her head with some kind of drapery before going to bed, and, he thought, must be possessed of a red lamp-shade—and the lamp must be flickering very much. There was a distinct playing up and down of a dull red light on the opposite wall. He craned out a little to see if he could make any more of the figure, but beyond a fold of some light, perhaps white, material on the window-sill he could see nothing.

Now came a distant step in the street, and its approach seemed to recall Number 13 to a sense of his exposed position, for very swiftly and suddenly he swept aside from the window, and his red light went out. Anderson, who had been smoking a cigarette, laid the end of it on the window-sill and went to bed.

Next morning he was woken by the stuepige with hot water, etc. He roused himself, and after thinking out the correct Danish words, said as distinctly as he could:

'You must not move my portmanteau. Where is it?'

As is not uncommon, the maid laughed, and went away without making any distinct answer.

Anderson, rather irritated, sat up in bed, intending to call her back, but he remained sitting up, staring straight in front of him. There was his portmanteau on its trestle, exactly where he had seen the porter put it when he first arrived. This was a rude shock for a man who prided himself on his accuracy of observation. How it could possibly have escaped him the night before he did not pretend to understand; at any rate, there it was now.

The daylight showed more than the portmanteau; it let the true proportions of the room with its three windows appear, and satisfied its tenant that his choice after all had not been a bad one. When he was almost dressed he walked to the middle one of the three windows to look out at the weather. Another shock awaited him. Strangely unobservant he must have been last night. He could have sworn ten times over that he had been smoking at the right-hand window the last thing before he went to bed, and here was his cigarette-end on the sill of the middle window.

He started to go down to breakfast. Rather late, but Number 13 was later: here were his boots still outside his door—a gentleman's boots. So then Number 13 was a man, not a woman. Just then he caught sight of the number on the door. It was 14. He thought he must have passed Number 13 without noticing it. Three stupid mistakes in twelve hours were too much for a methodical, accurate-minded man, so he turned back to make sure. The next number to 14 was number 12, his own room. There was no Number 13 at all.

After some minutes devoted to a careful consideration of everything he had had to eat and drink during the last twenty-four hours, Anderson decided to give the question up. If his eyes or his brain were giving way he would have plenty of opportunities for ascertaining that fact; if not, then he was evidently being treated to a very interesting experience. In either case the development of events would certainly be worth watching.

During the day he continued his examination of the episcopal correspondence which I have already summarized. To his disappointment, it was incomplete. Only one other letter could be found which referred to the affair of Mag Nicolas Francken. It was from the Bishop Jörgen Friis to

Rasmus Nielsen. He said:

'Although we are not in the least degree inclined to assent to your judgement concerning our court, and shall be prepared if need be to withstand you to the uttermost in that behalf, yet forasmuch as our trusty and well-beloved Mag Nicolas Francken, against whom you have dared to allege certain false and malicious charges, hath been suddenly removed from among us, it is apparent that the question for this time falls. But forasmuch as you further allege that the Apostle and Evangelist St John in his heavenly Apocalypse describes the Holy Roman Church under the guise and symbol of the Scarlet Woman, be it known to you,' etc.

Search as he might, Anderson could find no sequel to this letter nor any clue to the cause or manner of the 'removal' of the casus belli. He could only suppose that Francken had died suddenly; and as there were only two days between the date of Nielsen's last letter—when Francken was evidently still in being—and that of the Bishop's letter, the death must have been completely unexpected.

In the afternoon he paid a short visit to Hald, and took his tea at Baekkelund; nor could he notice, though he was in a somewhat nervous frame of mind, that there was any indication of such a failure of eye or brain as his experiences of the morning had led him to fear.

At supper he found himself next to the landlord.

'What,' he asked him, after some indifferent conversation,

'is the reason why in most of the hotels one visits in this country the number thirteen is left out of the list of rooms? I see you have none here.'

The landlord seemed amused.

'To think that you should have noticed a thing like that! I've thought about it once or twice myself, to tell the truth. An educated man, I've said, has no business with these superstitious notions. I was brought up myself here in the high school of Viborg, and our old master was always a man to set his face against anything of that kind. He's been dead now this many years—a fine upstanding man he was, and ready with his hands as well as his head. I recollect us boys, one snowy day—'

Here he plunged into reminiscence.

'Then you don't think there is any particular objection to having a Number 13?' said Anderson.

'Ah! to be sure. Well, you understand, I was brought up to the business by my poor old father. He kept an hotel in Aarhuus first, and then, when we were born, he moved to Viborg here, which was his native place, and had the Phoenix here until he died. That was in 1876. Then I started business in Silkeborg, and only the year before last I moved into this house.'

Then followed more details as to the state of the house and business when first taken over.

'And when you came here, was there a Number 13?'

'No, no. I was going to tell you about that. You see, in a place like this, the commercial class—the travellers—are what we have to provide for in general. And put them in Number 13? Why, they'd as soon sleep in the street, or sooner. As far as I'm concerned myself, it wouldn't make a penny difference to me what the number of my room was, and so I've often said to them; but they stick to it that it brings them bad luck. Quantities of stories they have among them of men that have slept in a Number 13 and never been the same again, or lost their best customers, or—one thing and another,' said the landlord, after searching for a more graphic phrase.

'Then what do you use your Number 13 for?' said Anderson, conscious as he said the words of a curious anxiety quite disproportionate to the importance of the question.

'My Number 13? Why, don't I tell you that there isn't such a thing in the house? I thought you might have noticed that. If there was it would be next door to your own room.'

'Well, yes; only I happened to think—that is, I fancied last night that I had seen a door numbered thirteen in that passage; and, really, I am almost certain I must have been right, for I saw it the night before as well.'

Of course, Herr Kristensen laughed this notion to scorn, as Anderson had expected, and emphasized with much iteration the fact that no Number 13 existed or had existed before him in that hotel.

Anderson was in some ways relieved by his certainty, but still puzzled, and he began to think that the best way to make sure whether he had indeed been subject to an illusion or not was to invite the landlord to his room to smoke a cigar later on in the evening. Some photographs of English towns which he had with him formed a sufficiently good excuse.

Herr Kristensen was flattered by the invitation, and most willingly accepted it. At about ten o'clock he was to make his appearance, but before that Anderson had some letters to write, and retired for the purpose of writing them. He almost blushed to himself at confessing it, but he could not deny that it was the fact that he was becoming quite nervous about the question of the existence of Number 13; so much so that he approached his room by way of Number 11, in order that he might not be obliged to pass the door, or the place where the door ought to be. He looked quickly and suspiciously about the room when he entered it, but there was nothing, beyond that indefinable air of being smaller than usual, to warrant any misgivings. There was no question of the presence or absence of his portmanteau tonight. He had himself emptied it of its contents and lodged it under his bed. With a certain effort he dismissed the thought of Number 13 from his mind, and sat down to his writing.

His neighbours were quiet enough. Occasionally a door opened in the passage and a pair of boots was thrown out, or a bagman walked past humming to himself, and outside, from time to time, a cart thundered over the atrocious cobble-stones, or a quick step hurried along the flags.

Anderson finished his letters, ordered in whisky and soda, and then went to the window and studied the dead wall opposite and the shadows upon it.

As far as he could remember, Number 14 had been occupied by the lawyer, a staid man, who said little at meals, being generally engaged in studying a small bundle of papers beside his plate. Apparently, however, he was in the habit of giving vent to his animal spirits when alone. Why else should he be dancing? The shadow from the next room evidently showed that he was. Again and again his thin form crossed the window, his arms waved, and a gaunt leg was kicked up with surprising agility. He seemed to be barefooted, and the floor must be well laid, for no sound betrayed his movements. Sagförer Herr Anders Jensen, dancing at ten o'clock at night in a hotel bedroom, seemed a fitting subject for a historical painting in the grand style; and Anderson's thoughts, like those of Emily in the 'Mysteries of Udolpho', began to 'arrange themselves in the following lines':

When I return to my hotel,
  At ten o'clock p.m.,
The waiters think I am unwell;
  I do not care for them.

But when I've locked my chamber door,
 And put my boots outside,
I dance all night upon the floor.
    And even if my neighbours swore,
I'd go on dancing all the more,
For I'm acquainted with the law,
And in despite of all their jaw,
  Their protests I deride.

Had not the landlord at this moment knocked at the door, it is probable that quite a long poem might have been laid before the reader. To judge from his look of surprise when he found himself in the room, Herr Kristensen was struck, as Anderson had been, by something unusual in its aspect. But he made no remark. Anderson's photographs interested him mightily, and formed the text of many autobiographical discourses. Nor is it quite clear how the conversation could have been diverted into the desired channel of Number 13, had not the lawyer at this moment begun to sing, and to sing in a manner which could leave no doubt in anyone's mind that he was either exceedingly drunk or raving mad. It was a high, thin voice that they heard, and it seemed dry, as if from long disuse. Of words or tune there was no question. It went sailing up to a surprising height, and was carried down with a despairing moan as of a winter wind in a hollow chimney, or an organ whose wind fails suddenly. It was a really horrible sound, and Anderson felt that if he had been alone he must have fled for refuge and society to some neighbour bagman's room.

The landlord sat open-mouthed.

'I don't understand it,' he said at last, wiping his forehead. 'It is dreadful. I have heard it once before, but I made sure it was a cat.'

'Is he mad?' said Anderson.

'He must be; and what a sad thing! Such a good customer, too, and so successful in his business, by what I hear, and a young family to bring up.'

Just then came an impatient knock at the door, and the knocker entered, without waiting to be asked. It was the lawyer, in déshabille and very rough-haired; and very angry he looked.

'I beg pardon, sir,' he said, 'but I should be much obliged if you would kindly desist—'

Here he stopped, for it was evident that neither of the persons before him was responsible for the disturbance; and after a moment's lull it swelled forth again more wildly than before.

'But what in the name of Heaven does it mean?' broke out the lawyer. 'Where is it? Who is it? Am I going out of my mind?'

'Surely, Herr Jensen, it comes from your room next door? Isn't there a cat or something stuck in the chimney?'

This was the best that occurred to Anderson to say and he realized its futility as he spoke; but anything was better than to stand and listen to that horrible voice, and look at the broad, white face of the landlord, all perspiring and quivering as he clutched the arms of his chair.

'Impossible,' said the lawyer, 'impossible. There is no chimney. I came here because I was convinced the noise was going on here. It was certainly in the next room to mine.'

'Was there no door between yours and mine?' said Anderson eagerly.

'No, sir,' said Herr Jensen, rather sharply. 'At least, not this morning.'

'Ah!' said Anderson. 'Nor tonight?'

'I am not sure,' said the lawyer with some hesitation.

Suddenly the crying or singing voice in the next room died away, and the singer was heard seemingly to laugh to himself in a crooning manner. The three men actually shivered at the sound. Then there was a silence.

'Come,' said the lawyer, 'what have you to say, Herr Kristensen? What does this mean?'

'Good Heaven!' said Kristensen. 'How should I tell! I know no more than you, gentlemen. I pray I may never hear such a noise again.'

'So do I,' said Herr Jensen, and he added something under his breath. Anderson thought it sounded like the last words of the Psalter, 'omnis spiritus laudet Dominum,' but he could not be sure.

'But we must do something,' said Anderson—'the three of us. Shall we go and investigate in the next room?'

'But that is Herr Jensen's room,' wailed the landlord. 'It is no use; he has come from there himself.'

'I am not so sure,' said Jensen. 'I think this gentleman is right: we must go and see.'

The only weapons of defence that could be mustered on the spot were a stick and umbrella. The expedition went out into the passage, not without quakings. There was a deadly quiet outside, but a light shone from under the next door. Anderson and Jensen approached it. The latter turned the handle, and gave a sudden vigorous push. No use. The door stood fast.

'Herr Kristensen,' said Jensen, 'will you go and fetch the strongest servant you have in the place? We must see this through.'

The landlord nodded, and hurried off, glad to be away from the scene of action. Jensen and Anderson remained outside looking at the door.

'It is Number 13, you see,' said the latter.

'Yes; there is your door, and there is mine,' said Jensen.

'My room has three windows in the daytime,' said Anderson with difficulty, suppressing a nervous laugh.

'By George, so has mine!' said the lawyer, turning and looking at Anderson. His back was now to the door. In that moment the door opened, and an arm came out and clawed at his shoulder. It was clad in ragged, yellowish linen, and the bare skin, where it could be seen, had long grey hair upon it.

Anderson was just in time to pull Jensen out of its reach with a cry of disgust and fright, when the door shut again, and a low laugh was heard.

Jensen had seen nothing, but when Anderson hurriedly told him what a risk he had run, he fell into a great state of agitation, and suggested that they should retire from the enterprise and lock themselves up in one or other of their rooms.

However, while he was developing this plan, the landlord and two able-bodied men arrived on the scene, all looking rather serious and alarmed. Jensen met them with a torrent of description and explanation, which did not at all tend to encourage them for the fray.

The men dropped the crowbars they had brought, and said flatly that they were not going to risk their throats in that devil's den. The landlord was miserably nervous and undecided, conscious that if the danger were not faced his hotel was ruined, and very loth to face it himself. Luckily Anderson hit upon a way of rallying the demoralized force.

'Is this,' he said, 'the Danish courage I have heard so much of? It isn't a German in there, and if it was, we are five to one.'

The two servants and Jensen were stung into action by this, and made a dash at the door.

'Stop!' said Anderson. 'Don't lose your heads. You stay out here with the light, landlord, and one of you two men break in the door, and don't go in when it gives way.'

The men nodded, and the younger stepped forward, raised his crowbar, and dealt a tremendous blow on the upper panel. The result was not in the least what any of them anticipated. There was no cracking or rending of wood— only a dull sound, as if the solid wall had been struck. The man dropped his tool with a shout, and began rubbing his elbow. His cry drew their eyes upon him for a moment; then Anderson looked at the door again. It was gone; the plaster wall of the passage stared him in the face, with a considerable gash in it where the crowbar had struck it. Number 13 had passed out of existence.

For a brief space they stood perfectly still, gazing at the blank wall. An early cock in the yard beneath was heard to crow; and as Anderson glanced in the direction of the sound, he saw through the window at the end of the long passage that the eastern sky was paling to the dawn.

'Perhaps,' said the landlord, with hesitation, 'you gentlemen would like another room for tonight—a double-bedded one?'

Neither Jensen nor Anderson was averse to the suggestion. They felt inclined to hunt in couples after their late experience. It was found convenient, when each of them went to his room to collect the articles he wanted for the night, that the other should go with him and hold the candle. They noticed that both Number 12 and Number 14 had three windows.

* * * * *

Next morning the same party reassembled in Number 12. The landlord was naturally anxious to avoid engaging outside help, and yet it was imperative that the mystery attaching to that part of the house should be cleared up. Accordingly the two servants had been induced to take upon them the function of carpenters. The furniture was cleared away, and, at the cost of a good many irretrievably damaged planks, that portion of the floor was taken up which lay nearest to Number 14.

You will naturally suppose that a skeleton—say that of Mag Nicolas Francken—was discovered. That was not so. What they did find lying between the beams which supported the flooring was a small copper box. In it was a neatly-folded vellum document, with about twenty lines of writing. Both Anderson and Jensen (who proved to be something of a palaeographer) were much excited by this discovery, which promised to afford the key to these extraordinary phenomena.

* * * * *

I possess a copy of an astrological work which I have

never read. It has, by way of frontispiece, a woodcut by Hans Sebald Beham, representing a number of sages seated round a table. This detail may enable connoisseurs to identify the book. I cannot myself recollect its title, and it is not at this moment within reach; but the fly-leaves of it are covered with writing, and, during the ten years in which I have owned the volume, I have not been able to determine which way up this writing ought to be read, much less in what language it is. Not dissimilar was the position of Anderson and Jensen after the protracted examination to which they submitted the document in the copper box.

After two days' contemplation of it, Jensen, who was the bolder spirit of the two, hazarded the conjecture that the language was either Latin or Old Danish.

Anderson ventured upon no surmises, and was very willing to surrender the box and the parchment to the Historical Society of Viborg to be placed in their museum.

I had the whole story from him a few months later, as we sat in a wood near Upsala, after a visit to the library there, where we—or, rather, I—had laughed over the contract by which Daniel Salthenius (in later life Professor of Hebrew at Königsberg) sold himself to Satan. Anderson was not really amused.

'Young idiot!' he said, meaning Salthenius, who was only an undergraduate when he committed that indiscretion, 'how did he know what company he was courting?'

And when I suggested the usual considerations he only grunted. That same afternoon he told me what you have read; but he refused to draw any inferences from it, and to assent to any that I drew for him.

www.ingramcontent.com/pod-product-compliance
Lightning Source LLC
Chambersburg PA
CBHW030244180626
46810CB00008B/3281